THE HAUNTED WRITER

RAMONA BLOOM

ONE BOOK MEDIA

One Book Media

www.onebookmedia.ca

The Haunted Writer: *Based on actual events*. Names may have been
changed to protect the innocent. In certain cases incidents, characters and
timelines have been changed for dramatic purposes. Certain characters
may be composites, or entirely fictitious.

❀ Created with Vellum

For my daughter, who begged me not to write this book,
for fear that evil may return...
May I remind you, The Light is so much stronger.

"But the Lord is faithful.
He will establish you,
And guard you,
Against the evil one."
2 Thessalonians 3:3

Based On Actual Events.

I feel her watching me.

It's an intensity of a stare that only registers in my soul. I try to shake it off, leaving a trail of lights illuminating behind me. I hope that the brightness will diminish my awareness but it only works to remind me of how scared I am.

I have shelved this project more times than I can count and yet here I am again, finding myself doubling down, struggling to recreate all that I have burned.

I think she will leave me alone if I write her story. I am her friend. *Then she reminds me that evil has no friends.*

"For we do not wrestle against flesh and blood, but against the rulers, against the authorities, against the cosmic powers over this present darkness, against the spiritual forces of evil in the heavenly places." Ephesians 6:12

Our family built a large cookie cutter brick house in a new flourishing subdivision in a quiet lakeside community. Out of love, my husband Rick, always worked hard to give me whatever I wanted, the envy of my friends, a stay at home mother who could choose the carpets, the design, the cabinetry- it is my dream after all, to build new for there is something about the fresh smell that a new home breathes. We keep our other home as revenue property, all part of my master plan, even though tenants make it difficult.

We have two children, Marianne and Celeste. I always wanted a sister, someone I could play with, so I was happy I could do that for them. I enjoy their imaginations, their playful nature, it amazes me how very different they are. Marianne will mix solutions and create mysterious science-like projects in her room or the kitchen; Celeste will create little businesses like a store to sell us things we have already bought or an amusement park in the backyard and charge the neighbourhood kids a quarter for an afternoon *at the circus.* They remind me of how I was without the fascination for paper.

I always knew I wanted to be a writer.

Learning my letters and practicing cursive was something that seemed second nature. In the first week of second grade, my teacher Mrs. Appleby stroked the words across the chalkboard in crumbled powdered chalk, "My Summer Holidays". It was her way of getting to know us, or rather how well we could write. In excitement, I was determined to write the best story ever. On yellow lined paper, I wrote my first story and gave it to her out of love for my teacher. My classmates struggled to write one page and yet I had written nineteen. In grade five, I wrote my next *The Haunted House*.

We already make friends with the neighbours. It is easy to do when children ride tricycles up and down the sidewalk, parents lingering not too far behind. We only know one other couple in this lakeside town and that is Steve and Linda. They entice me to come out. I figure it's because I am a stay-at-home Mom and they know I need a change of scenery. I jump at the chance for adult conversation.

Entering the doorway of the darkened pub, I feel a tinge of guilt for running out the door so fast leaving Rick bewildered in the driveway. Now, I stand as a fish out of water amongst a room full of drinking fish. They hover around tables in loud chatter. The water's edge from the deck off the back of the pub draws me in and I long to stand there under the moon. Moon conversations are essential with a busy family life.

"Ramona! Over here!"

At a corner table, Steve and Linda greet me with wide smiles and a wet beaded drink rests on a coaster. I fall into their arms like warm butter and it feels good. "Hi, good to see you!" To me, they feel like family. Clumsily, I nearly knock over the drinks while placing my purse next to me. I peel off my jacket, the moon still calling me.

"Why are you wearing a jacket?" Steven teases. "I know, I know." We laugh about this. I will never get used to it, jackets have always been necessary where I come from, but not in these parts.

We chat about the move, the house, the children, and their children- whom I haven't seen in a while. I will no doubt be shocked by their size when I see them again. They promise to come over with the children, maybe next week. I will have to tell Rick to make sure he is home. In the midst of our small talk, I am surprised when Steve waves someone over. He pulls out a chair too. Did they invite someone else? For a moment, I am hopeful that it is Rick, but it isn't and I try not to look disappointed. How could he come?

"Ramona, this is Pierre... Pierre- Ramona," says Steve. "Hello." Should I extend my hand for a shake? Do people do that anymore? "What'd you have, Pierre?" He signals to a petite waitress. "Oh, just a Bud is fine." I watch Steve flirt with the waitress, looking at Linda as he does. She shrugs. I can tell she is used to this. Rick would never do this I am certain. Steve is even as bold as to ask for her number and then lets out a boisterous laugh as if it's a joke.

Pierre has a curious stare on me. When I notice, he peers into my eyes almost in a creepy way and then he looks down at the table between us. Is he depressed? In contrast to Steve, he is very serious.

"So, this is the writer I was telling you about," blurts Linda. Writer? What? What has she told him? My eyes grow wide in a panic motioning to Linda to stop with this. I am barely a writer and feel embarrassed more than anything for my lack of accomplishments. I have nothing published. I think about my half written stories. Has Linda read anything? No, I don't think so, I haven't shared them with anyone.

As a child, I turned my room into a library, taking the books I owned and creating pockets in the back of them so that I could slide a piece of paper to stamp on with the due dates just like they did at the school library. Anyone who came to visit was invited to browse in my library. It didn't consist of more than a bookshelf. Often, I reminded my mother that her book was overdue and she owed me a penny. I could buy two caramel candy squares for a penny. My father was less than enthused by my pursuit to write. With the high expectations he had for his only child, I always dreaded the days when he would pour himself over my report card and lecture me for hours about what he read there. I was only good at English and Art. Pierre reminds me of the way my father looked at me, the oozing disappointment, the *I'm not so sure what to do with this one. The writer... sure you are... how wonderful.* "What books have you written?" The judgements continue... I swallow hard. "Um... nothing yet... I am not published." I don't want to mention the enormous collection of rejection letters in my desk drawer. The funniest one with just a swift reply, "No... no... no." I sip my beer like therapy. Steve orders another one, an excuse to talk to his darling.

"Pierre has a story for you!" says Linda, with great excitement.

"Oh, ya?"

"Oh, ya," she mirrors. "A real good story!" She beams like a headlight.

With his soft grey eyes, he peers into me. Why does he keeping looking at me like that? Am I worthy enough to hear it? I'm just a stay-at-home Mom out for a beer. He is a rich man with a big loud stare and a presence that commands authority. It's his eyes though that intrigue me most for I can see that they harbour great secrets.

"It's a bestseller, right, Steve?" adds Linda.

Steve chuckles in his larger than life way.

They all know the story but me.

"So, what's the story?"

Pierre sits with his arms folded, his beer untouched. He stares off into the distance like he isn't even with us anymore...and then he is... and then he isn't.

"I told him, if anyone can write this story, I know Ramona can. She is really good!"

Linda keeps chirping. I realize how much she likes to talk. I am happy to just sit here and relax, enjoy the quietness but she will have no part in this. When I look at Pierre he gives me a knowing smile... Yes, she does talk a lot. I can feel something else lurking under the surface between our glances. I can feel it, like a pulse... like a danger... like the calm before a storm. Pierre needs another drink, he isn't ready to share yet. "It all started-" begins Linda.

"Honey, let Pierre tell the story," interrupts Steve. We order another round as I glance to the back deck to wonder if the moon is still there in all its glory. Maybe it is up for conversation? Finally, after numbed by alcohol, the room a slight buzz, our pupils dilated, the pub lights dimmer, Pierre opens his thin lips and word by word describes the chilling details. I feel a tingle in my fingertips and imagine keystroking words to a page. He tells me all that has happened within the walls of his family's farmhouse. It isn't too far from here. There are no explanations as to the strange occurrences happening in the home. He doesn't live there anymore, but his parents do. Still struggling to make sense of it, goosebumps rise on my arms and legs.

"Is this for real?" I ask Linda. I know Linda wouldn't lie to me.

"I swear on my kid's grave, Ramona, this is all true! No word of a lie, right Pierre?" she says.

Pierre nods yes with a heavy frown. I can see the regret and horror in the lines on his face.

"So, what do you think, Ramona? Are you going to write it?" asks Linda.

... and so it begins.

Married longer than he can remember, Charlie Livingston, loves his wife, Wilma, with a deep sense of duty and honour. She has stood by him through the war, waiting for the love of her life to return so they could begin their lives together and start a family. Everything that he does is for Wilma including building this family legacy on the property that she had inherited from her grandparents. They work the land hard, adjourned with animals and crops, now just a distant memory from the hard life they once cultivated. The grass now overgrown, blows wildly; an electric buzz mysterious in its origins overwhelms the mind if you think about it too much, announcing the heat stuck in the air. The farm never sleeps and carries a subtle cry of something lurking.

Charlie, bound to a chair, can't keep up with the grounds. The years have been cruel to him and slowly he deteriorates; the skin clings to his fingers like thin wet paper, revealing knuckles of white bone from years of struggle, a decay of the mind and spirit. He knows better than to travel outside when it rains for his wheels track in an endless supply of mud despite his desperate attempts to wipe the wheels clean. The less work he makes for Wilma, the better, but often he has to check on the septic system, the well, the damage after a wicked storm. It bothers him more than anyone will know that he can't climb to the roof and fix shingles or poke around like he used to.

The attic carries all kinds of strange noises even though no one is up there. The walls whisper to the lurking, in the rise of moving shadows on painted canvas, displaying mysterious contrast to the blankness of the unknown, dancing between light and dark. Charlie talks it down to pesky squirrels, old pipes, creaking wood. If only he could investigate.

He wheels himself over to the bottom of the stairs and closes his eyes to listen. In the silence of closed lids, he can hear better. The stairs speak back to him as if it is ridiculing his disability. You can't climb me! You're an imbecile! You useless old man! You are confined to the first floor forever!

Peter often urges his parents to sell the family farm for he believes here on the fringes of the city, this piece of land is worth a small fortune and he tries desperately to convince his brother, Pierre, that this is the best thing for their aging parents. Wilma will have no conversation about this and that is all the confirmation Charlie needs. "Nope, we won't do it." "But Dad, it's too much for you." Peter! What did Peter care? He barely visits, a disappointment for being a first born son, too good for any of them. He never did like the farm. Determined to make it work, Charlie resists calling Pierre or Peter for anything. He can take care of things himself. The wretched prison of a chair tells him otherwise.

Sadness rises in Charlie's chest when Pierre leaves. He spins around in his chair to look at Wilma who is crying too under her friendly wave on the front porch. It is hard to admit how much you need your grown children.

Over the years, Wilma has been less attentive to things around the house, perhaps she is bored by them. She no longer irons linen like she used to or hangs clothes on the line, she rarely bakes. The smell of baked bread is something Charlie always loved and Wilma always made the best. He never complains. Folding a piece of bread out from a store bought bag with his shaking hand is much easier than making one from scratch even if it doesn't taste the same. Sandwiches have become his best friend, his lonely friend. He does have a best friend, a dog named Pal, an Australian Shepherd who has worn out a good old spot on the floor by the window where he can stick his speckled nose through the curtains at the slight sound of a car. A wagging tail is what most people meet when they enter.

The Pilkerton's live just down the road. They are wonderful neighbours. Henry Pilkerton always has a soft spot for Pal and often carries treats in his pocket; Joanne Pilkerton will drop by extra things if they have gone to the store. Instead of buying one carton of milk, she will buy two. She loves Charlie like her own but Wilma takes a bit getting used to. Wilma doesn't like too many people and she has no regrets about stating so. She is suspicious of any one kind unless it's the kindness of Charlie, the colouring returning to his apple cheeks when he sees her. She takes every opportunity to remind him of all she does for the cripple.

"She's at it again, isn't she?" says Joanne. Joanne has dropped by one afternoon with coffee. Charlie waves his hand in a 'Oh, don't you worry about that,' kind of way. "It makes her happy."

Having a father as an alcoholic, Joanne has little sympathy for any one who chooses to ruin their lives. She would be furious to know that Henry has gone to the liquor store for Wilma on more occasions than he cares to mention. Wilma flips Henry a twenty dollar bill for his efforts, she is generous when it comes to her drinking. Charlie appreciates Henry when he collects the empty bottles too, he is tired of hearing the constant rattling and tripping over the growing collection by the back door.

They always know when Wilma will begin her attic retreat. It is the only time she thoroughly cleans the house with meticulous precision. Spotless to a fault, she makes sure the bathroom towels are lined just so, the soap dish free of scum, the garbage scrubbed and emptied, the dishes clean and sparkling and put away nicely, and not a speck or line left on the floor. Even Pal has multiple bowls of water and heaping hills of dog food. Charlie loves a clean house but dreads the smell of bleach for he knows that his time with Wilma is dwindling. When the thirst appears she possesses an attitude that carries a complete lack of understanding, void of any love, taking on a personality that isn't even Wilma anymore.

In the dark, Charlie lays on their bed missing her warmth beside him. He listens to this thing. She drinks her pain, the never forgotten offences that no one cares about, how it spills from her lips in the bitterness of slurred banter. The words become louder and angrier and then quieter again, only to repeat. Who is she talking to? Sometimes he wonders if he is supposed to answer? Oh well. What does it matter? She is drunk. The smell of cigarette smoke leaks through the floorboards, how must they be stained in yellow drippings? If he is lucky, she will pass out and he can get some peace.

One night on another one of her drunken escapades, Charlie wheels himself to the bottom of the stairs. Pal lifts his head in a sympathetic notion. They know that Wilma chooses to drink in the attic because it is the only place Charlie can't go. He can't beg or ask her for anything, the attic is her special haven away from all the responsibilities of life... But, he can't hear the television. He is about to say, "Will you shut up!" Instead, he rolls out to the front porch with Pal. Pal rests his furry head on his knee with the slight whimper. Charlie pats his head. What a good boy! "Oh, well, Pal, what are we going to do?" Pal looks like he is contemplating this in the soft expression of a dog's eyes. "A day or two and she'll be back to her old self." They are soothed by the stillness in the night air, the only thing moving is the rustling of leaves. Even if he feels all alone, at least he has Pal.

A few days later, just like clockwork, or perhaps the fact that she has run dry, Wilma emerges from the attic, her heavy steps making the announcement. She acts like nothing has happened, like she has just returned from grabbing something upstairs. From not having showered for days, she reeks of sweat and stale smoke and the sourness of alcohol. Charlie doesn't care. He is just happy to have his Wilma back! She presents him with a plate of smiling eggs, just the way he likes it and perfect strips of bacon. He gulps down the bites as she watches, almost in a creepy way. She eventually has a plate of her own, swallowing back the guilt that has consumed her for she knows no mention of her drinking is a kind reward.

The old television set hums hot, anchored between them like old friends. It fills in the easy silences they both love. They laugh and ridicule the contestants on their favourite game show and take turns guessing the answers. These are the happiest times with Wilma. As the days pass, her attentiveness to him begins to decline. She becomes grumpy and grumpier and makes her generous plans to ensure she has her full liquid supply. Charlie doesn't under-stand why she needs this? She never used to be like this? He tries hard not to ask for too much, why does she have to leave? No matter how nice he is, even if he is stuck between the chair and the bed, or the toilet, no matter how hard he tries not to be a bother, even rolling over to the television to change the channel to something she will want to watch, she will still find an excuse to hide herself up in the attic. How he dreads the sound of them clanging empty bottles falling to the floor. She is slowly killing herself and there is nothing he can do.

"Mom, what are you doing?"

"Writing a story."

Celeste rests her adorable little face at the edge of my desk, hungry for attention. Her big brown eyes look up at me and then the computer screen.

"Can I read it?"

"Oh, I didn't know you could read?"

I am delighted by her interest. The other day I tried to read her a story I was certain she would love, full of beau-tiful pictures and the animals she loves, but no, Celeste is not interested in books. Picking up the piece of paper from the kitchen table with my small black typed letters, she perks her head up and clears her throat like she is giving a speech to the world- "Blah, Blah... blah, blah... " Celeste stops to smile and then continues, "Blah blah blah." I snap the pages from her little hands! Rick pokes his head from the living room with a laugh- "Oh, she can read!" "Very funny!" "We all know your writing is blah- when's lunch? I'm starving." "Are you hungry too, Celeste?" She has to think about this. "Is it candy?" I fold her up in my arms and tickle her, "Is it candy! Is it candy!" She squirms and giggles. "You don't need candy!" "Yes, I do!" Her attempts to convince me fail.

Over lunch, I complained to my husband. The children run off with their grilled cheese sandwiches and cucumber slices because they want to eat outside. They constantly open the screen door because they forget something and all my hard work whisks up in the breeze of the doorway to fly around the kitchen in a dance. The children multiply and soon all the neighbourhood children are there spilling through the doors, sending my loose leafed pages to blow outside. "This is ridiculous! How am I supposed to write?" Rick burps and rubs his tummy. "That was good, thanks." The children come in once again and run around me, dodging each other from the game of tag they play. They flail their arms around me, stretching for the other. "You're it!" "No, you're it!"

I gather the dishes and collect what is left of my un-numbered manuscript. I don't know how many pages blew out the door. They are all hand written. I know I can't write in the kitchen. I need someplace private, some place where I can leave my papers, where there is no wind, no distrac-tions... and that's when I clean out our enormous walk-in closet. Politely, I tell my husband that his clothes have been moved to the hall closet. To my surprise, he is cooperative.

P al has taken off into the woods again. It isn't the first time. For a better part of an hour, Charlie calls out but that damn dog is nowhere to be found. The storm clouds are rolling in the distance, there fullness rising out of the abyss with a darkened undertone that warns danger. With the hint of rain against the whip of a cold snap, Charlie wheels himself to the end of the porch feeling the chill right down to his bone. He is more sensitive to cold than he used to be but he needs fire. The fireplace chokes with smoke, it would not light, preferring to remain in the dark. He needs wood. Wilma would like a good fire, he will have to make it to the shed.

Pierre has built a ramp for him as a way to keep his hopes up, many years ago. It bridged off the left side of the porch and then ended in the softened earth where the grooves widened from prior passage. Charlie tries to veer himself more to the left but he always ends up stuck in the deeper grooves. He will have to remember to ask Pierre if he can extend the ramp to the shed. His arms are weaker now and it is hard to wiggle himself free. Most often he rests in shallow breath, thinking about calling Wilma. He hates doing this. It makes him more determined to try again so he won't have to. Too tired, he rests again. If she comes out and sees him, maybe she will help. He closes his eyes in a squint, feeling the burn in his chest. Just one more try. He can do this. With one more great push, he raises the wheel out of the groove and up on firmer soil. The chair easily rolls to the shed now and relief washes over him.

In a sudden jump, Pal springs from the opening of the shed's door.

"How in the world did you get in there?"

Charlie looks around but doesn't see anyone. Is Wilma here? No..no, that's right... Wilma went to the store. He hopes she doesn't get caught in the rain.

Against the wall of the shed are stacked pieces of wood. Pierre has cut them nearly perfect and stacked them neatly. With great effort, Charlie wheels himself into the shed, the smell of beautiful pine inviting him in with fragrance. Pal shakes at the doorway, his four legs mostly but he is not cold. Out of the blue, he barks, making the log fall down, slipping from Charlie's grasp.

"God damn dog! What are you barking at?"

Charlie listens for a car. Is Wilma back?

What are you barking at?

Pal keeps barking and lunging forward.

There is nothing there.

"Knock it off, Pal!"

Feeling a pain in his side, Charlie leans over the chair and tries again to pick up the log. It is out of his reach. Why is life so hard? He wishes he could kick it with his feet but they are extensions of dead wood. *You are useless.* His fingertips graze just the top of the wooden log.

Out of nowhere, the shed's door slams shut.

Pal barks from the other side.

Charlie sits in darkness.

Thunder cracks, so loud, that it makes Charlie jump. It is pitch black in the shed, so much that he can't even see his own hand in front of his face.

"I can't leave you alone for a second!" Charlie is surprised to see Wilma, the logs nearly tipping off his lap. She opens the door and grey light spills in, her face drenched in rain, water so hard it plummets down to cause pain.

"I thought you might like a fire Wilma."

"I thought you might like a fire," she mocks him.

He can see the plastic bags dangling from her arms, her vodka bottles poking out. Thunder growls and lightning shines against her face like a villain. Violently, she tugs at his chair. "Careful, the log!" She nearly trips on it before she can wiggle it loose from under him. "Now how on earth did you get that there?" She pulls it out, finally, and adds the log to the heaping pile of wood on his lap . "OK, let's go." Carefully, she pushes him out of the shed. He holds onto the precious logs so they won't roll off his lap. "Watch this groove, here, Wilma." "I know, I know." She is more concerned about her bottles breaking, the way they clang around in the wind. She misses the spot and quickly Charlie sinks in the mud just at the edge of the ramp, just what he was afraid would happen. "I wish you wouldn't do this, Charlie! I wish you would have waited for me!" Charlie hangs his head low. "I'm sorry." She tries to push him out of the mud but can't. The more she tries, the worse it seems to get. They are both soaking wet, water spitting from their mouths. "You make it so hard for me, Charlie! So hard!" "I'm sorry. I'm trying not to."

She pushes him again.

He isn't going anywhere.

"I can't do it," she says in defeat. "Ok, take the logs." One by one, she throws them on the porch. One smacks against the window and cracks it. He can see that she is mad- real mad. Mud leaks up to her ankles and her shoes are covered. "If I wanted a fire, Charlie, I would get the logs myself." "I'm sorry.""I'm sorry! I'm sorry! That's all you ever say!" Pal wags his tail from the porch. He has successfully dodged all the flying logs. "I'm going inside." In a huff, she walks up the porch, paying no attention to Pal, and slams the door behind her. Pal barks from the porch as if encouraging Charlie to try again.

Charlie slumps.

This is impossible.

He shivers in the cold, helpless at the side of the house. The shed's door bangs in the wind like a marching drum. The rain whips at his face in violent lashes. If he listens close, he can hear her chunky steps on the stairs climbing to the attic, teetering on her ability to shuffle the extra weight she carries, careful not to disturb the precious bottles that cling to her arm. Despair fills his stomach when he looks up to the attic window for a light turns on although dim. He knows he could be stuck here for some time. Soon, he will hear her drunken banter against the thick of the storm.

The attic can hear her too and is the only one who will listen... until even it has had enough.

"WHY IS MOM IN THE CLOSET?"

"She is working on a book."

"Ya, get the hint, she doesn't want to be disturbed."

"She's a closet writer!"

They laugh. I can hear their voices from outside the door and the small knuckles of Celeste knocking. "Mommy... Mommy... Ma ma!" "What?" No answer. And then they leave, finally, and come back... and leave again.

Later, Rick barges through the door and scares me! Of course when I scream he finds this hilarious. "Are you writing the scary part?" My heart is pounding. He reaches over to grab the fan I have on my desk. In protest, I grab it from his hands. "The kids want it." "No! This is my fan! Go buy them one." "Why? We have a fan?" "No, I have a fan. You don't!" I put it back on my desk. "But we are hot." "So... go get some ice cream or something."

The children with their radar ears hear the word ice cream and already begin to celebrate.

"Ice cream! Ice cream!" "Thanks," says Rick, sarcastically. I laugh. Well, that's what he gets for trying to take away my beloved fan. "Bring me back one." "No, it will melt. Come with us." I look back at my screen... not now... I am in the flow...

THE STORM SPILLS like a falling river, rain remnants like drops of blood staining skin leaving a residue. To Charlie's relief, Henry stops by because Wilma has forgotten her purse in his truck. Eagerly, he runs over to Charlie at the side of the porch not knowing that he has been there for hours. Puddles hide the depth of the wheels sunk in mud and with great difficulty, Henry pushes him up and out. Charlie is most grateful and could almost cry. He hopes that Henry will stay and he goes to the kitchen to put on the kettle.

"Oh wow, look at all that mud," says Henry. Already,

there are spiralling tracks on the floor leaving a trail every-where Charlie has been. Henry looks up the stairs, his foot on the first step. "I can get Wilma?" "No...no... let her be." They know she is drinking again."Let me do it then?" "No, no, don't worry. I'll be fine." "Are you sure? Are you sure you're going to be OK, Charlie?" I guess this means he isn't staying? "I'll be fine. I'll be sure to let Wilma know you brought her purse."

The storm ravages on. Charlie watches Henry run out to his truck as Pal stands beside him at the window. A slim man like that can move fast in the rain. The kettle whistles but Charlie has lost all interest in tea. They give a friendly wave as Henry pulls out, the headlights blinding.

Charlie rolls over to the television, violently slamming his hand against it when it refuses to work. He can hear the sound of spinning bottles on the floor above him, the usual clank of her stupid bottles. How much does she drink? Does he really want to know? It is best to think about Wilma the way she was when she was young, selfless and beautiful.

WHAT! The power goes out!

I am typing!

Boom!

Out!

Just like that. No warning. Is all my work gone? I sit in the dark with a blackened screen realizing just how dark a closet is without windows. The power flickers back on as if deciding whether or not it should. I power up the computer, grateful for some light, relieved to see it has autosaved, and I continue.

THE POWER GOES OUT!

Thunder cracks!

Charlie jumps!

Pal shakes beside him with a bit of a cry. He follows him as Charlie wheels himself to the bottom of the stairs. "Wilma! The power's out!" He waits. Patiently. He listens. "Wilma? Do you hear me?" She doesn't answer. He can only hear the sounds of bottles spinning on the floor or dropping from the ceiling? "You better not have any candles burning up there? You'll burn the house down!" More than anything, he wants her to come down. He doesn't care if she has liquor on her breath, he just wants his Wilma. She must have passed out early tonight? He tries one more time, "Wilma! You hear me?"

Silence.

Eerie silence.

A rising darkness descends down the winding staircase, glutinous in its consumption of any light until each step is lost in its growing presence. There is a moving shadow but it only makes its appearance in the flash of lightning. It does not look like the shadow of Wilma. Charlie knows what her shadow looks like. Pal whines. He hovers near the front door, aggressively scratching at its corner. Charlie slowly moves back from the stairs, rolling gently. He turns slightly to face Pal. "No, I'm not taking you outside! It's storming out there!"

Distracted by the dog, he doesn't see it coming.

A blunt force causes his wheelchair to abruptly push back.

He doesn't understand it because there is nothing there that he can see.

It pushes him back again.

Pal barks uncontrollably.

The chair violently turns to the left, nearly spilling him out of it. It then jerks to the right. When it lifts on its back wheels, Pal runs and hides. The cold sensation of someone clenching his arm leaves Charlie feeling light headed, a deep shivering of sorts right down to his spine, although in those bones he has lost all feeling. He spins in a blurred confusion, swirls of room pass his eyes, no wind to help him catch his breath, the shaken brain scrambled.

It doesn't stop.

It won't stop.

Burning vomit comes up his throat but he swallows it back down tasting the stench. It comes up again but this time spills from his mouth, splattering on every wall as he turns. From the spin, he passes out.

The chair bounces.

The bounce makes Charlie bite his tongue until it is raw. All of the wheels make contact with the floor. The wheelchair rolls and slowly hits the wall. Charlie is stooped over, dry mouth, tongue out, eyes rolled to the back of his head.

A small marble rolls out across the floor. It traces the mud patterns left from the wheels of the chair, thoughtful not to get stuck behind any chunks of vomit. Pal, afraid of the marble, runs from it. Slowly, it circles back, never stopping.

Even the dog knows the marble is not just a marble.

5

In a flow of words, I know I have made the right choice to write in the closet. I don't care what anyone says, even teasing me about being a closet writer. Just this weekend alone, I have plowed through almost ten thousand words. I have never written this much in one sitting before- it's like I can't stop! I lose all track of time, sometimes writing into the dead quiet of the night as my family sleeps, the excitement of the story writing itself. As my fingers pounce the keys, I don't notice a gruesome black spider with its knobby needle like legs. It dangles from the crevice opening of the attic above me. In fact, I don't even realize that there is an attic opening here in the closet. If I did, it is doubtful I would write there. So enthralled in my work, I don't see it dancing above me, swaying in the breeze of the fan. Quickly, it descends and falls in the soft spot between my breasts, as if that is the target. It hides inside my shirt and I look down when I feel it move. What is that? Something has touched me! A spider! A spider! In horror, I scream. I jump! I tip over the chair and run out of the closet, nearly falling down in the doorway.

My family stands holding their ice cream. They are stunned by how I run down the stairs to the open foyer screaming. "What is it?" "What's wrong?" "A spider! A spider!" The children look to the floor to see if they can see one crawling. "Where?" "It came down on me... " I am breathless. I can hardly speak. "In the closet!" I don't feel it anymore. I don't know where it went. "It was huge!" I keep dancing as if I am still shaking it off. Rick laughs hysterically for he knows how much I hate spiders. "I told you, you should have come with us." "Ya, Mom" echoes the children.

That was the last time I wrote in the closet.

I made Rick remove everything from the closet and I never returned there. He was happy to have the fan back. Even returning for clothes, I would look up and feel uneasy when I looked up towards the attic opening. Could it be a doorway to the unknown?

IN THE MORNING, Charlie awakens. Why is he in the chair? He can smell vomit. How did that get there? He wheels himself to the bathroom to clean up. His head hurts. He flicks on the light switch. That works just fine. Did the power go out last night? He tries to recall. He can't remember much... let's see.. I was stuck outside, then Henry came... then what happened? The sun streams through the windows as if pronouncing that the looming darkness is forgotten, a fresh start to what could potentially be the brightest day, if only that were true.

Charlie wipes his mouth and washes his hands. He takes

a tall glass of water from the tap, not caring that the cup is filthy. He wants more. He isn't sure where Pal is. Strange. Usually that dog is not too far behind. He rolls himself to the living room. Where is Pal? The stillness is eerie. Rays of light shine through the curtain to spill on the floor revealing a terrible dried mess. He would have to find the mop. Hopefully Wilma will not come down until he does. "Wilma! Wilma!" The stairs still taunt him. He resents this. He remembers the times when he ran up those stairs, both flights, in less than twelve seconds. Even if he could crawl up there now and make it to his old bedroom, there is no way he could crawl up another set of stairs to the attic.

With great difficulty, Charlie attempts to mop up the floor. It turns into a big soupy mess and he wishes he had never started. Boy, oh boy, will Wilma be mad when she sees this! He throws the mop and decides on breakfast. He calls for Wilma one more time. Maybe the smell of bacon will entice her down. It does entice Pal! Pal slowly comes out from the back closet. "There you are, Pal!" They enjoy their breakfast together, Pal getting a little more bacon than usual- Wilma's share.

In the afternoon, Charlie turns on the television. He plays with the antennas, trying to get it just perfect. There is a baseball game today and he doesn't want to miss it. Pal sits beside him with perky ears. For a second, they both think they hear footsteps coming down the stairs. At least he has changed his shirt and he looks good for Wilma. They look, but she never comes.

Later in the evening, Charlie falls asleep. He decides it is best to go to bed. He is tired of calling for her. He thinks about how she left him outside. He would still be out there if it wasn't for Henry! Would she leave him there that long?

He thinks about this and picks up the phone. "Ya, it's Charlie... Can you come over... I'm worried about Wilma."

"C'MON, that's funny! A spider falls on you while you're writing a horror story." "No, Rick, it's not funny!" He continues to laugh with a jump out to scare me. I roll my eyes. "I've already quit! I'm not writing it!" "Just because of a little spider?" "It fell from the attic! The attic!" "That's even funnier!" "I don't think it's funny at all, Rick!" "Oh, c'mon! It's just a little spider." I fold my arms in a pout. I am disappointed that I can't write this... that I am bothered by this. I feel like I am disappointing everyone around me. "I'm not a horror writer anyways, I write romance." "Romance is boring." "Not to me. The characters feel real-" "The characters are real! This is a true story!" "I know, Rick! That's what makes it worse!" I cuddle up to his arms and we snuggle on the couch. This is our time, my most favourite time of the day when the children are in bed and we can just be together. I feel safe here.

"I think it's just your writer's imagination," Rick continues. "I didn't imagine the spider, Rick." "So, that's a coincidence. A funny one." He laughs. "It's not just that... the other day, no one was home and I- Oh, never mind." "You what?" "I heard someone upstairs." "See, that's your imagination. It's working in your favour!" "But I heard someone walking. This isn't an old house, Rick. It's brand new!" He clicks the remote to change the channel. "I think it's funny that you are so scared."

He is distracted by the return of his favourite television program and we don't talk anymore about it. I guess I am scared, very scared. Maybe Rick is right? Maybe this is all just my writer's imagination? I am writing things that are scaring me. I'm not used to this. Maybe it will be good? If it scares me, it may definitely scare my reader? This is a good thing, right?

I sit back down and think about this. I feel better. I have disposed of everything again. That's Ok.I can start again. But there are definitely holes in the story? Things I cannot explain? I don't know how the story is supposed to go? I am stuck. I go over the facts of what I know- this happened and this happened, but then what? I close my eyes. I try to connect with the old farmhouse. I try to see it in my mind's eye. I speak to it. I ask it to show me. *Show me what you look like? Show me how it feels? If you want me to write this, show me? I am your friend.* And then... I wait.

The worst is confirmed.

IT IS TOO much to take when the paramedics bring out the body, its blanket draped over her. Charlie clenches his hand across his mouth trying to not let the sob escape him. His beloved Wilma is dead. She has finally drank herself to death.

It surprises him when the detectives relentlessly demand to speak to him asking the same questions over and over. "Can you tell me what happened that night?" In his grief, he struggles to remember. He doesn't want to tell them that Wilma left him outside. He wants his beloved Wilma to be remembered for the Saint she is. When Henry gives his account, they question Charlie even more. You said this, but

Henry claims this, twisting it all up until they all are confused. He closes his eyes to concentrate, fragments of memory dislodging anything he can explain. "Were you sick? Where did the vomit come from? Did killing her make you sick to your stomach?" Silence seemed permissible but only to those who believe that Charlie could never be capable of such horror.

When Pierre arrives, he is angered by the presence of the police. His father is clearly shaken and visibly exhausted. He has had enough! No! He is not! He isn't going anywhere! But there are more questions that need answers and nothing makes sense. The way they find her body lying on the floor of the attic, like she had fallen off a building- her arms flailed to the side, her legs bent unnaturally, a look of fright on her face. They discover through the autopsy that every bone in Wilma's body is broken. Not one bone, or a few, but all. How could this happen? They scour the residence for evidence. "How long have you been in that chair?" "Fifteen years or so." "And you really cannot walk? Stand?"

The questions send Pierre into a rage. They ask for his alibi too, and everyone... everyone that they know. "We have reason to believe that this wasn't a natural death," the detective reveals."What do you mean?" "We believe your mother was murdered." "Murdered? How? Like an intruder or something?" "Your father seems to have no recollection of what happened-" "He is old and senile! What do you expect?" "We believe your father could be responsible for the death of your mother?" "How? He can't climb the stairs?" "He is the only one that was here." "That's all you got? C'mon! This is ridiculous!" "Has he ever been abusive to your mother in the past?" "What? No!" "Have you ever seen them argue?" "What? No! I'm getting a lawyer!"

Charlie Livingston is prosecuted and charged in the

connection for the death of Wilma Livingston. His children sit helplessly as he is rolled away to serve the remainder of his sentence.

They have a good lawyer.

At least, it was only manslaughter.

6

FFffffffffffffffffffffffffffffffffffffffffffffffffffffffffffffffffffffffffffffffffffffffffffffffffff
FfffffffffffffffffffffffffffffffffffSdfasdkflasalskjfwptu9-9opl;

I turn on the computer and open the document to find someone has been typing in it. Immediately, I call Marianne and Celeste into the dining room, to which they both deny ever having touched the computer. The dining room is now my makeshift home office. I have a large window that I can open for air although I still have my fan blowing on me. My family knows that the dining room is off limits and with the exception of the girls playing on the computer, I believe they respect this for the most part.

I delete the endless pages of entries and notice that even some of my work has mysteriously disappeared. What the? Didn't I save this? I think about the power going out? No, it was saved? I let in a deep sigh. Well, maybe this is a good thing. I think about ways I can rewrite it differently that might be better.

. . .

I TAKE the girls to school but I can't wait to come back to write. I sprint home after I drop them off at the teacher's door, dodging conversations with other mothers who linger around the school grounds. But, at home, once sitting down at the computer, I am blocked. What was I going to write again? I have so many bouncing thoughts and now none of it is coming to me. Where did it go? Why didn't I write it down when I was thinking about it? Feeling restless, I get up and mop the floor and empty the dishwasher. Then, I attempt to sit back and write. Wow. This is crazy. It is not like me to be blocked like this. Struggling still, I get up and throw a load of laundry… now… let's try again. I convince myself that the only talents I possess are the delusions of inadequacy and an overactive imagination that exist to only impede my sanity. Rick is right, my writing is blah. I should just give up.

The house is quiet. I like it quiet. It feels uncomfortable quiet and I am not sure why I find this uncomfortable? Why am I listening for something? Expecting something? Out of the corner of my eye through the kitchen doorway, I see something move. I look. It's a black marble. It rolls slowly, bouncing against the bottom of the kitchen cupboard, spinning. The hair on the back of my neck rises- this is just my writer's imagination, right? I am waiting for something to happen, it does, and that's it! This is all in my mind. I feel jittery. I try to focus on the pages but the sound of the imaginary spinning marble distracts me. Focus, Ramona, focus. Just write. Ok, let's do this.

"Isn't that crazy?" says Linda.

We ordered another round.

Pierre has to go, he has to work in the morning but he shakes my hand and says it was nice to meet me, all the formalities. I don't get the feeling that he is expecting too much from me, especially the next bestseller, and it is a relief.

"Couldn't they argue that he was in a wheelchair? Like how would he get up there?"

"They tried," adds Steve.

"Do you think there's a chance he could have done it?"

"Ramona, there is no way! And you know what else happened?"

"What?"

"Honey, she knows, Pierre just told her."

"I know, I know… I just can't believe the six years, six months and six days thing-"

It's there.

Something is here!

I can see a face staring back at me.

It is over my shoulder, showing in the reflection of the computer screen.

My heart is in my throat.

I turn around.

I don't see anyone.

I look back at the screen.

Nothing.

I am sure I saw something. I feel very uneasy. *This is just your writer's imagination! This is just your writer's imagination!* I tell myself this to calm my nerves. When this doesn't work,

I try to be rational. I walk from room to room. If something is here, I want to know. I collect the dirty dishes left in rooms, pick up toys and laundry. I don't see the marble on the kitchen floor anymore. See, it is just imaginary! I don't see a marble anywhere. This is great! There is no marble. I check Celeste's room. She has so many toys. Her stuffed animals are all aligned neatly on her bed. They stare at me in a creepy way. Marianne's room is opposite, and not clean at all. She has no stuffed animals but I find my expensive perfume and other things I thought I lost, like my new lipstick. No marbles. I think I am losing my marbles.

I scare myself when I walk past a large mirror and something moves. *It's you, you idiot!* Rick is right. This is just a case of my overactive imagination. I try to put the uneasiness to rest. Still, I can't shake the feeling that something is here. I pack my stuff up and go to the local coffee shop. Maybe there I can write.

7

Confined in a prison cell is not what Charlie envisions in his later years and yet here he is, one of the oldest prisoners. The animals locked away in here are not in for petty crimes and when he claims he is innocent, they laugh- "You keep telling yourself that, Grandpa!" There is no use talking, or talking to anyone for that matter including the onset of lawyers his sons keep sending. What good is a lawyer who can't even win a simple case! Based on his physical deterioration, he can't believe they would have found him guilty of anything but the defence was able to paint a very good case against him based on the many years of perceived spousal abuse. Charlie scuffs at this! He resents anyone who speaks badly about his Wilma, especially when his sons are in earshot. Sure, she wasn't perfect but he certainly wouldn't call it abuse. A man can do horrible things in a rage, even a cripple, they say.

At random parts of the day, Charlie weeps into his pillow. Sixty some years with the woman he loved, and now, now she is gone. He smothers the sounds seeping from him so as not to disturb the others or bring any unnecessary attention to himself. Terribly depressed, he doesn't groom himself. The other prisoners complain about the old man smell, he is a rolling green cloud. Still, he will not bathe. No one can get through to Charlie and he is placed on suicide watch. He refuses to meet with visitors. Get on with your own life! Don't waste your time coming here. This suits Peter just fine, but not Pierre, it only makes him more angry, more desperate to get him out of here. Oh, don't you go wasting any more money on those useless lawyers! I'm an old man now. What does it matter?

Pierre needs money. Peter is not willing to contribute. The legal fees are compounding. He is referred to a high profile real estate agent named Manny, a business acquaintance of Peter. Peter wants to get a sense of what the family farm is worth in today's market.

Manny pulls up in his gleaming Mercedes and a nice suit, afraid to soil his shoes when he steps out in the mud. Pal jumps out of Pierre's truck and sniffs around the familiar grounds, threatening to jump on Manny who wants no part of a friendly dog's dirty paw greeting. They enter the house and leave Pal outside on the porch. It has the feeling of a museum, stepping back in time. "My father didn't use the furniture much." Manny creaks across the wooden floor boards. He looks through the curtains with his finger, expecting to see Pal there but he isn't. He notices the old leaking windows, the black mold around the frames, the dated decor and smell of rotting wood. Browsing unimpressed, the bathroom is in deplorable condition according to Manny's standards. Manny stands with his hands in his pockets. "I have to be honest with you, Pierre, there's not much value here in the house... but the land.. The land is worth something!" "What do you think I could fetch for it?"

They walk outside to the porch and Manny is thoughtful about his answer. "How many acres again?" "Fifteen, give or take." Manny shrugs, "I don't know... probably 1.4." Pierre nods in agreement. This is the number he thought but was hoping for more. Slowly, they move off the porch and walk around in the blowing grass. "I would clean all this up." That would be good."

Manny sees the shed and for some reason wants to go there. Pierre points to the ramp-

"Watch yourself there, I built that ramp for my Dad... he's in a wheelchair." "Oh, and where is your Dad now? Did he pass?" It is then that Pierre has realized that Manny is not that close of a friend to Peter, and knows nothing. "No... no... he is still alive."

Manny opens the shed just to take a look and quickly cuffs his hand around his mouth. He takes a deep step back. Pierre lunges forward to see what is wrong. Inside, floating in the middle of the air are thousands of flies buzzing in the formation of a dog. The overwhelming stench makes their eyes water, it is wicked and sour at the same time. The men swat at the flies as they disperse, breaking apart to buzz around their heads. At the swallowing of flies, they run to their vehicles for shelter.

Manny calls Pierre on his cell phone from inside his luxury car. "What was that?" "I have no idea?" "So, what happens now?" Manny inhales sharply. "I guess it is just a matter of meeting your father, unless you or Peter have power of attorney?" "No, no, we don't.." "Ok, no problem. Where is your Dad now? The seniors lodge?" Pierre thinks to maybe leave this part of the conversation to Peter but his pressing eyes through the window entice him to speak- "In prison actually." "Prison? For what if you don't mind me asking.""He was charged for murder but he didn't do it."

Manny looks at Pierre through the car window not sure if he is understanding everything correctly. "Maybe you should talk to Peter." Pierre eyes dart around for Pal. Where is that dumb dog? "Murder? Did it happen here?"When Pierre doesn't answer, Manny gets the idea. Politely, Manny starts his car with a wave of the hand, and hangs up the phone. It doesn't take him long to drive off the property.

"MARIANNE?"

I stopped her in the hallway one morning.

"Do you have any marbles?"

"Marbles?"

"Ya, marbles. Do you like, have any?"

"Why do you want marbles?"

"Never mind."

"I would like some marbles, Mom."

8

The day Charlie is released from prison is a good day!

He surprises himself that he has lasted this long, there are times he imagined that he might pass. It wasn't that bad, really, once he became used to the routine and in some ways, he might miss it? It still stings to think about Wilma. He misses her every day and he supposes that will be true for the rest of his life. The thought of returning home without her is unbearable, but life must go. Someday, it will be his time. He hopes someday soon. As Pierre drives him home he wonders if his son has thought about this- that one day he will be gone.

The Pilkerton's still live down the road. Charlie is happy about this. He hasn't seen them in gosh, how long?

"Do you think they think I did it?" "I don't know, Dad, that's a good question. You'll have to ask them." Charlie frowns- "I suppose." "I know you didn't do it." "Thank-you, son."

They pull into the driveway and Charlie waves his hand up-"My God, look at this place!" "I tried to clean it up a bit for you, Dad. Mowed the grass and stuff." "I can see that, thank-you so much." "Bet you'd never see this place again?" "That's for damn sure." It is then that Charlie notices... He is expecting him to be standing on the porch wagging his tail. "Where's Pal?" Pierre hesitates. There is no easy way to say this. He turns off the engine as his father's eyes closely observe. "No," cries Charlie. "He was old, Dad." Charlie bites his trembling lip. He sobs in big long breaths. "I know, Dad, I know." Pierre rubs his back. "He was such a good boy, he really was." "We can get you a new dog, Dad." "No. No..." "Here, let me help you get out." Pierre lifts him from the truck into the chair. Charlie wipes his wet eyes with the back of his hand, gripping the chair as Pierre pushes it up the driveway to the side ramp.

Pierre's eyes fall on the shed as they pass with a nagging sense of doom. He thinks about how odd it was to see those flies in the shape of a dog the day Pal disappeared? A horror he will never tell his father.

After some time, the sun retreats. Pierre feels pained that he has to leave but he just cannot stay any longer. "Are you sure you're going to be alright, Dad? It doesn't sit right leaving you here." "Ah, don't you worry 'bout me, Pierre. I'll be fine." "I'll come by tomorrow." "Right-O".

Charlie waves to him from the porch as Pierre backs up his truck. He sits there for a bit, like old times. The porch offers the temporary illusion of a peaceful mind: the way the darkened greenery can still look beautiful in the haze of night; the way the crickets sing like they could love you; the way white butterflies joyfully zag in a friendly gesture of hello, ignorant to the crows who watch them. Aside from the crickets, it is deathly quiet, inside especially. Charlie looks to those stairs. He wouldn't see Wilma come down those anymore. An overwhelming loneliness permeates the room.

The house seems different and yet the same. He thinks he knows who did this, what is to blame but he doesn't want to think about it now. *Rest in Peace Wilma.* He would like to do the same. In his growing tiredness, he makes his way to bed. He can lunge out of the chair quite easily and roll into the bed. How good it will feel to be in his own bed with the familiar linens and smells.

He falls asleep almost instantly. A nice deep sleep. As he is sleeping, the wheelchair moves on its own.

It rolls to the end of the bed- out of reach.

9

As time goes on, I become more obsessed with this story.

I think about it often, what really happened? How could it have happened? I close my eyes and concentrate clearing my mind to what it will allow me to see. In my mind's eye, I see a little girl. She is no older than six years old. She has long dark hair and is dressed in an old fashioned red dress with tiny white polka dots in the fabric. Her shoes are old fashioned and she is thin with knobby knees. I can see her playing in the attic. She walks over to the door and tries to open it but it is locked. I think she is a sweet little girl until she turns her head to look at me. Her stare rips terror throughout my body. I open my eyes. It is her eyes that remain with me most, how vicious they are, black spools of darkness that tell me she is anything but human. I try to catch my breath.

I think about what I might find at the library? Perhaps I can see the history, if there is a little girl that had lived there prior? One day, after I drop the girls off at school, I drive

down to the downtown library and search the archives.
When I come up nearly empty, I think about what else I can
do. Maybe it is time to take a visit to the old farmhouse?
Rick thinks this is a good idea. He wants to come too, but I
tell him that it might make it more awkward, that Pierre has
not mentioned that I would be bringing anyone.

I knock.

I wait a long time.

I remember that Charlie is in a wheelchair and
answering the door takes time.

I hold on to what Pierre has said: *A visitor might do him
good. He would like that.* When he doesn't answer the door,
my mind begins to overthink- what if he is dead in there like
Wilma was? What if I find his body? What if? What if?
What if? There goes my overactive imagination again, but
what if it isn't? Then, the door opens.

"Hi, I'm Ramona? The writer? Did Pierre tell you?" He
can barely look up from the strain in his neck. I am
surprised that a man in his condition is living alone. "Wait
on the porch." He slams the door. I don't have a nice
welcoming feeling. The porch creaks and I look around. I
can't imagine anyone wanting to stay here. Minutes later he
comes out, struggling to put on a jacket. I help him fold his
arms into the sleeves, he is out of breath from the effort.

"You live here alone?" "Last time I checked." He offers
me a smile although small, more like a hint of one. I walk
across the porch trying to fill in our awkward silences. The
house looks as creepy as I imagined it to be and I wonder
what the inside looks like, if it is any better?

"Do you think your house is haunted?" I blurted this out.
Maybe it isn't the best thing to say. "Think! I know!" His
deep set eyes hide behind frisky eyebrows, long crooked

strands of silver leading nowhere but wiggle upon expression. He doesn't elaborate.

"Thanks for talking to me. I really appreciate it." "Not my idea."I smile at him, trying to create a warmth between us. Slowly, his eyes soften. "So, you're a writer, are you?" "I do like to write." "What's your book called?" "Well, I'm not published as of yet. I hope to be! Soon!" He nods, not that impressed. "This is a nice piece of property." "I'm sitting on a gold mine!" I look at his chair as he says it, and then look away. "Must be hard to get by in one of those?" "It has its challenges, that's for damn sure." I wish there was somewhere I could sit. I think about the front steps but they are crooked with poking nails and I don't want to hurt myself or fall through.

"So, I did some digging!"

I pull out my story pages, some photocopies, and the notes I have taken. Most of all the photocopies I have are of the area, it's history, and old newspaper postings that describe it. It doesn't amount to much but shows my commitment. "I think there was a girl here... a little girl that used to live here."

"You find that in your research?"

I swallow hard. Not exactly. How do I tell him that I see her when I close my eyes? He gives a knowing nod and points up towards the side of the house. "She died in the attic." "What?" You mean there is a girl? I am right? I feel happy about this. She is helping me to write her story. "How do you know?" "My wife told me." Has she seen her too? "The family don't talk about her much, such a shame, you know." "What happened to her?" "I think, and I could be wrong... that she fell from the attic window." "Fell or pushed?" Charlie shrugs. "I don't think they treated her right." "Aren't you afraid to stay here?" "Death would be a mercy."

I think about those words a lot: *death would be a mercy.*

I walk to the side of the house where the attic window is visible the most. I take notes of the peeling paint, the dull wood, the cracked windows, the arched dirty window in the attic. Hopeful for a glance of something, I fully expect to see her standing there looking down at me. I have prepared myself mentally for this moment. *She is not there.* I don't see her, and I feel disappointed.

Charlie has gone inside now. I hope that I haven't upset him. I sit in my car and think about what he has told me. I feel inspired and pull out my notebook to write. It flows so beautifully and I am certain that this is the missing piece to the story. I know there is a little girl. I know what she looks like. I know what the house looks like. Maybe we are friends? I am helping her. I understand her. Just then, a horrendous sound comes at me in an attack! It's the sound of flapping! I look, stunned to see a large black crow just outside my car window. It lunges its blackened beak, adamant to peck at the pores of my skin. The sound of its frantic wings flapping is amplified by its close proximity to my left ear. I scream! I roll up the window quickly! My notes have flown all around the car. Even with the window sealed, it still tries to peck at me through the glass. Its eyes are evil. Although I am sheltered, I am not any less fearful. I am an intruder and not welcome here, this is clear. Even the birds know it. They caw harshly in offence with a nasal ring that echoes in my mind long after I depart the haunted lands.

"You think this is funny, Rick?"

"I think you should stay overnight," he jokes, although he is serious.

I slide the roaster in the oven.

"You can end your story half finished- what happened to the writer? We don't know?" I think about this. That is a good idea, I will give him that. Rick is always good with ideas. "I'm not writing this! A crow tried to get in my car!" "You'll have to put that in the book!" "Forget it! I'm not writing it."

… until I did.

⁓

BASEBALL SEASON IS over and the beginnings of a Canadian winter hang in the shortened days of a late wet fall. Charlie grows comfortable in the silence, his ears losing their purpose over time, but his eyes, no, now they are seeing too much. He knows something is there with him, something up in that attic, something that killed Wilma. It is easier to pretend that evil doesn't exist. These sounds… these shadows… the spinning bottles on the floor… how he hated those most of all. It still continues with her gone. It is easier to pretend that this is just Wilma. Yes, sweet Wilma, still here and alive. He will be forever stuck in her memory.

He speaks to Wilma often. Rolling himself to the bottom of the stairs, he asks very politely if she would like a sandwich.

The scrape of a chair drags across the floor above.

"Wilma? I can hear you."

When this begins, it's as if the walls become alive: the knocking of old lead pipes, the creak of hissing wind through widened gaps of floorboard. The house takes on a whisper of the unknown but we all know, it knows. It knows more than it is willing to say. Parts of it hint to a darkened past, like the peaked windows on the third floor attic, how those panes whisper if you listen close enough. The window is covered in mildew and grime making it hard for anyone to see anything for certain. Perhaps that's the way it wants it-like a whisper, faint and fleeing, like a wheelchair that refuses to remain still even when empty. Charlie devises a clever plan. He ties the chair to his bedpost. This has seemed to work so far.

One night, he awakens because he is cold. The sheets and blanket have been snapped off, tumbling to the side of the bed, leaving him to shiver. He notices his wheelchair is not there and when he lifts his head to look down towards his feet, he jumps to see something. His eyes focus in the dark, squinting. It is something sinister... something... Oh, wow! It is Pal! A smile wipes across his face, how happy he is to see him. He stretches his fingers towards him but Pal growls, a hint of teeth beneath his gum line. How very peculiar? Pal has never been vicious before? "Pal? What has gotten into you?" The dog continues to growl with a threatening bite and for this he does not untie him.

In the morning, the wheelchair is back to where it was and tied just the same, to the bedpost with a string loose knot.

Pal is not there.

The Pilkerton's have stopped by, "Charlie? Oh, there you are. We are just on our way to the store, do you need anything?" "Yes, Pal is out of dog food." "Pal?" Joanne raises her eyebrows, nudging Henry in his side. He motions to 'just go along with it' for they both know that Pal is dead and Charlie has forgotten. "Oh, right, the dog food." "Yes, you know the kind he likes. The purple bag." "Yes, we know Charlie, we will be sure to get it." "I don't think Wilma needs anything. She has stopped drinking, you know." "OK, Charlie."

They leave feeling disturbed and instead of going to the store, they find themselves in Peter's office waiting for a chance to speak to him. "We're concerned for your father." "My father?" "Yes?" "What's wrong?" "He is terribly confused about things." "Did you talk to Pierre?" "We are afraid he won't listen. It's time Peter. Your father needs to go into a home." Peter has known this for quite some time. He listens carefully to all they explain about Charlie's mental deterioration- the loss of days, the confusion. "I'll see what I can do."

Charlie is surprised when Peter shows up at the house. He calls him Pierre and then Peter and then Pierre again and Peter can see what the Pilkerton's mean. His father is worse, much worse than he thought. He coerces him into a nice country drive and some drive through lunch. "Let's just go look, Dad." Not much he can do, he isn't driving.

The building screams institutional with its boxed in windows, the sliding front doors, the large flower pots with beautiful bursts of colour, the fluorescent lighting overhead, the stale smell of old bodies and sitting urine. How very badly Charlie wants to go home. They show him a room, not much larger than his living room. It has a bathroom, a bed, a modern television- "they have cable, Dad." In the center where all the hallways lead is a large open area with small easy wipe tables, light spilling in from the skylights above. The staff seem courteous and friendly, busy and unattached. "What do you think?" Charlie shrugs. It is nice but it is like being in prison all over again.

A frail woman passes by in a wheelchair. She jumps at the sight of Charlie and quickly squeezes his arm. Her fingers are cold, but her grip is strong. She digs into his skin- "666!" They rush to sedate her. Even the staff are surprised by her strength. It is her expression that scares Charlie most, her eyes wide and bulging, her gaping mouth. Peter keeps pushing the chair like nothing happened.

"We are so sorry about that, Mr. Livingston," a staff director has come running out as Peter walks to the car. She is attractive. Charlie is sure Peter will think so. "I can assure you that this is completely out of the ordinary. Are you OK Charlie?"

"I am fine."

He states this simply, as in a 'I told you so, I didn't want to come here', folding his hands in his lap. There are scratches on his arm from her nails.

Pierre is furious when he learns about the visit. The two brothers almost end up in a first fight on the porch. Charlie is just too tired to say anything. "He is not selling! You can't take him from his home!" "This isn't about the money, Pierre!" "Bullshit!" Pierre does agree with one thing... their father needs help and that's when the onslaught of personal care assistants begins to arrive.

The first is Jenny. She looks barely old enough to drive, Charlie thinks, as enters bright with smiles and a bouncy ponytail. She spends more time on her phone than anything else, annoyed by the poor reception and even more annoyed to learn that Charlie has no internet connection.

The second is Wanda, then Julie, then Mavis or Marilyn-Charlie forgets. There are so many that he cannot recall, or even if they have come at all, but then there is his favourite-Anna. She is older too, but still much younger than him, a short lady with a soft sympathetic smile, the kind you could find warmth in when you gaze into her brown eyes which he most often tries to do. She cares for Charlie the way others never could, even better than Wilma, and for this, he even feels a twinge of guilt to admit he might like Anna better. She doesn't speak that well, in English, and he wants so much to talk to her about things, to ask her questions about her life, her family. It's her gestures of gentle touch, the way she takes time to be present, combing the few strands of hair he has over a balding head. It is not about the hair but being in the moment, their eyes connecting in the mirror, the way she makes an old man smile when he has nothing to smile about.

10

The snow has fallen and it takes me three hours to shovel the driveway.

I am determined to do this, tired of being cooped up. We drive to Steve and Linda's house, on the other side of the lake, bringing piping cups of coffee and hot chocolate for the children. Linda's house is small and feels messy because of the clutter. We stand on broken tiles and lean against nicks in the walls slowly squeezing through hallways so we can sit somewhere comfortable. She lets her children run wild and I can see why the house looks this way but I do not say anything for I adore her children like my own. For a few hours, my children get the freedom of running wild too and I can see the excitement in their eyes, for this is not my house and I do not make the rules.

She asks me about the book, how it is coming along. I share my progress vaguely, downplaying the fear I feel when I talk about it. I can still remember the crow. It has haunted me. Goosebumps graze my arm and I am amazed at all the peculiar things that I have imagined. I wonder if I can share these with her or would she think I am crazy? I tell her about the girl... not that I saw her in my mind before I went to the old farmhouse, but that there is a girl, one who had lived in the attic and the possibility that her evil spirit is still there.

"Do you think she is out for revenge?"

Linda thinks about this. "Revenge?"

She is unsure what I mean, I can tell.

"You know, anything or anyone who comes in contact with her?"

"Like a poltergeist?"

"Ya, I mean, maybe she is angry."

"I don't know, I don't even want to think about it."

But, we both are thinking about it. Would she be angry with us? Would we be on her hit list too? We hear a loud crash! It is not our children because they are in the other room. This sound has come from the back door. Linda and I scream, grabbing each other, and then laughing at the same time. "Boy, Ramona, are we paranoid!"

It is Malcolm, her oldest son.

With great struggle, he is bringing a bicycle through the doorway, chunks of ice hanging off of it. It has wide tires, nothing like I have ever seen before. "Don't be bringing that in here," says Linda. "But Mom, where am I supposed to put it? His nose and cheeks are red from the outside. "I don't care, but not here." He rolls his eyes and takes it downstairs. "Outside!" she yells but he does not listen. "That's quite the bike." "Oh ya, he rides it come rain or shine." "Or snow!"

The Thing is hunched over.

IT HAS JUMPED up on Charlie's bed like a crouching tiger only Charlie can't feel her there, his legs are its playground. Her mouth is tainted in his blood with bits of shimmering glass, she chews on, so tasty. She uses the sharp edges of the bottle to tear into his skin leaving deep abrasions and cuts up and down his legs and feet, the flesh ripe for feeding. Dangerously, she cuts near the veins with precision for meat but never lets him bleed too much for torment is much more fun.

When he awakens, he has no idea how those cuts have got there, or that they are even there at all until Anna notices them when she bathes him. In horror, she cries, dipping the bath sponge in the brown stained water and rinsing it, careful not to disturb the crusty scabs. In other spots, she scrubs him down to the bone, hopeful that he might regain his sensation.

They do not talk about it.

He would if she could understand the words.

She doesn't have to explain. He can see that she knows. It's the fear in her eyes that he recognizes, and she doesn't come back.

A new personal care assistant takes Anna's place but Charlie refuses to bathe. He doesn't even care to know her name. She cooks for him so he will take his medication, *must take with food*. It trembles on the table, a lonely pill, and he finds it difficult to grip it with his fingers. He asks about Anna. Will she come back? Is she well? But no one knows.

When this one leaves, her car does not start. She is stuck there waiting for a ride. Charlie watches from the porch, swatting the pesky flies that land on his face. There is nothing wrong with her car, it's just the way this place breathes, and then she too, does not return.

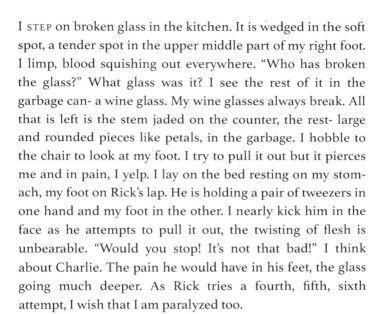

I STEP on broken glass in the kitchen. It is wedged in the soft spot, a tender spot in the upper middle part of my right foot. I limp, blood squishing out everywhere. "Who has broken the glass?" What glass was it? I see the rest of it in the garbage can- a wine glass. My wine glasses always break. All that is left is the stem jaded on the counter, the rest- large and rounded pieces like petals, in the garbage. I hobble to the chair to look at my foot. I try to pull it out but it pierces me and in pain, I yelp. I lay on the bed resting on my stomach, my foot on Rick's lap. He is holding a pair of tweezers in one hand and my foot in the other. I nearly kick him in the face as he attempts to pull it out, the twisting of flesh is unbearable. "Would you stop! It's not that bad!" I think about Charlie. The pain he would have in his feet, the glass going much deeper. As Rick tries a fourth, fifth, sixth attempt, I wish that I am paralyzed too.

Wilma is upset with him

.

"Oh, C'mon now, Wilma, don't be like that."

Another bottle shatters against the wall. He can hear it break upstairs in the attic.

"Come watch, Wilma. Our show is on."

It is Anna. He has been thinking about her too much, Wilma doesn't like that. The damn TV is not working. Last night, it turned on by itself and now it is not working at all.

"Wilma, the TV is not working."

"I'm sorry, Wilma, I'm sorry!"

He would hear then, in his mind. "You're always sorry! That's all you ever say!"

Instantly, the television turns on and he wipes his eyes from the tears, Wilma has forgiven him. How wonderful she is. He laughs at the contestant, "You stupid idiot! It's a 'P'" He pats the arm of the couch, as if Wilma is there. An indentation compresses itself on the couch and he finds it odd that he cannot move his hand, it is pinned there. Oh well, Wilma wants it that way. She likes to hold his hand. He waits until the television decides to turn off and then he is free to go as he pleases.

RICK HAS PURCHASED a new television set. He stood in line for hours in the early morning, waiting with the others, just to be the first ones to arrive when the store's doors opened. They only had ten television sets for their blowout sale, he was lucky to get one. We surround the large screen in anticipation, Rick pulls it out of the box, the children jumping. It is like going to the theatre but never leaving home. The children are more excited for the empty box and what they can make out of it, so I bring out the markers and cut holes for them where they want. This keeps them busy while Rick sets up the surround sound. The surround sound overwhelms me and I realize that I do not like it. It sets my nerves on edge, in overstimulation- I prefer it only in the theatres. Rick loves it. I can hear the explosions and gunfire, the action music trailing into my headspace while I am one room over in the dining room. I wonder if I can write with the noise.

A neighbour finds our old television set at the curb side. I tell him it does not work, there are lines in the screen but he is happy to have it. They tell me a week later, it is perfect and that there are no lines at all. I give them other things, whatever they want, from the stack of electronics in the garage that Rick intends to recycle. They turn on and off randomly on their own, or don't work at all.

Rick has to leave, although it is late.

He pauses the movie and says- "I'll be back" like Arnold Schwarzenegger. He has to bring something over to one of our employees. I am delighted that the house is quiet, listening closely as I hear his truck backing out of the driveway. Finally! I can write in peace. The children have gone to bed hours ago, wow, this is great! I get about three sentences in when I hear the television set turn on. It scares me. It is blaring loud!

I walk into the living room, through the kitchen, searching for the remote.

I cannot find the remote.

Then, it pauses all on its own? Not another broken one?

I stand bewildered. Maybe Rick is playing a joke on me... maybe he is sitting in his truck with the remote. I check the driveway, the street through the window, but his truck is gone. The frame on the television is stuck on a yelling face, someone is angry. I feel uneasy. I walk back to the dining room and sit down in my chair. Now I don't feel like writing. Maybe I can get into it again? I read over what I have written and think about what to write next. Oh, yes, now I know where I am...

Then, the television turns on again.

This time, I am mad.

I march back to the living room, mostly afraid but trying to disguise it with anger. I feel the hairs rise on my skin. This time, I unplug the television.

I look around the room with a circular gaze. It is empty.

Not one shadow. And then, I hear it! Giggles! Relieved, it is just my children. They are hiding behind the couch, the television remote in their little hands, one of their heads pop up to reveal themselves. "It was you!" They throw the remote at me and make a run for it but I catch them, they squirm to get away, screaming in delight. They cannot stop laughing. "We scared you! We scared you!" "No, I thought it was Dad?" "No, you didn't! You thought it was a ghost!" I chase them upstairs and we laugh and talk until Rick finds us all asleep in our bed.

11

The Pilkerton's check on Charlie every few days.

One Sunday night, they sit down to a family gathering with extended family when the phone rings. Joanne has made her speciality, fried chicken. "No problem... OK then, thanks Pierre." He hangs up the phone. "Is Charlie alright?" "Um.. he's not sure. He wants me to stop by... been calling for days, no answer." "I can't believe he still lives there?" their family comments. "Ya, you and me both." "Not for long, I'm sure."Joanne can see the growing anguish on Henry's face. Charlie, always like a Dad to him. "You wanna go over there now?" "Ya...do you mind?" "Go ahead, bring him some chicken."

Looking out his windshield, Henry doesn't get a good feeling when he pulls up in his pickup truck. He sees some kind of movement of shadows within the house, mostly from the upper floor. This confuses him. Could Charlie climb the stairs after all? Wouldn't that be something if he had fooled him all these years? Then he thinks about the time Charlie was stuck in the mud... No... he is not able to climb... to walk. How crazy that he would think so.

Slowly, Henry approaches the house.

A warm plate of chicken accompanies his hand when on the porch, something stings him and he drops the plates. The chicken rolls down the steps, it's skin gets caught on a nail. The plate breaks and makes a crushing sound beneath Henry's boots. Henry checks his finger. It looks like some kind of sting. He pulls it out, whatever it is. How on earth do wasps survive this time of year? No... it couldn't be a wasp?

Something moves at the corner of his right eye and he has to look not once but twice. It doesn't move this time but he is certain it just did. It is Charlie's wheelchair. It sits on the edge of the porch. There is no one in it. An eerie feeling that something bad is going to happen rises in Henry's stomach and he doesn't like it. He is never this afraid! Why is he now? He keeps his eye on the chair and walks to the door without hesitation. What would Charlie be doing without his chair?

The door is locked.

Surprised, he rattles the knob.

The wheelchair turns slightly as if to watch him.

Henry jumps off the porch.

He walks to the side of the house until he comes around to the back.

He bangs on the back door.

"Charlie! Charlie! It's Henry!"

This door is locked too.

He waits and listens but hears nothing.

"Charlie? Are you there?"

Feeling a sense of urgency, Henry breaks the glass. It is cracked anyway. He lets himself in through the back door, holding his wrist close to his abdomen for now, not only does he have a sting on his finger but also a cut of the wrist.

Charlie is not in his bedroom.

He is not in the living room, the kitchen or the bathroom. Through the window view, the wheelchair creeps by but Henry is too busy looking for Charlie that he does not notice.

The front door blows open.

Henry closes it, certain it is the wind.

"Charlie!"

After searching the entire main floor, he realizes that Charlie is not here. Puzzled, he knows he can't go too far without his chair. He looks up the steps and wonders... could he? Would he be up there? Blood drops fall from his wrist onto his boot. He presses his fingers against it, to stop the bleeding. He really doesn't want to go up there.

Down the stairs, a small marble bounces as much as a marble can. Nothing is ever as loud as a spinning marble, sporadically in motion with no control of its own, an announcement to defy logic. It circles around him before falling into the drops of blood splattered on the floor, leaving a bloody trail as it rolls further. How he hates this house. He runs up quickly, so fast, like a shot of adrenaline boosting his jump. At the top, Henry is lightheaded. Does he need stitches?

Quickly, he searches the second floor.

THAT EVENING IS PARTICULARLY difficult to get the children settled into bed. I run the bath water hoping some warm bubbles will help, bribing the children who don't like to bathe with fun squeezy toys to squirt. They know the routine- bath, pajamas, story, drink- and anything else they can think of to delay the inevitable. I tuck Marianne in first even though she is the oldest because she is the most cooperative. I give her a slight tickle and she climbs into the blankets and we talk about all the fun things we will do tomorrow. The sooner she goes to sleep the sooner it will happen, I remind her.

"Mommy! Mommy!" Celeste calls out from the other room. "What?" "Mommy! Mommy!" This continues for a while. I roll my eyes and Marianne giggles. "Why does she have to be so difficult?" Marianne shrugs with a smile for we all know she is the angel child. "Mommy! Mommy!" "I better go see what your sister wants." "She wants to stay up!" "Yes, Marianne, I know." "Good night." "Good night."

I turn off the light but make sure her night light is on because she is still afraid of the dark. It's a mood lamp that dances in purple blobs. Celeste's room is right next to Marianne's. I can see her moving from under the blankets. "Mommy! Mommy!" "What is it Celeste?" I say this in an annoying tone because she always tests my patience and this time is no different. "There's a monster under the bed!" "There's no monster, Celeste." I bend down beside her bed to show her, I am sure this will make her feel better, and that's when I see it! Under the bed! A face void of sun, the pale remnants of what once was- *it is her*! *The Thing!* Her limbs are gnarls like crossed tree roots, her dull hair covering part of her darkened face and she has a vicious raspy voice not of a girl at all- "*there's a monster on the bed*," she mimics.

In a frightful jump, I am up against the bedroom wall.

I knock over Celeste's bookshelf and all that stands on it.

The blanket is flat and wrinkled. The bed is empty. Where is Celeste? Her stuffed animals stare at me with their wide stitched eyes, mouths open, frozen like they are in fear too. One touches my foot and I panic thinking something else is touching me. I struggle to catch my breath. *Wow, do you ever have an imagination! This is not real! This is not real!*

Immediately, I leave the room.

I walk near the bathroom and see Celeste in the mirror. She is singing and playing with her toys in the bathtub.

I take a deep breath.

*I*s this Celeste? Or is it her? Calm yourself down! This is just your mind! You have spent a lot of time writing today. That's all this is. Still, I am scared. I usually just see her when I close my eyes but not ever when they are open. I can't control this and I do not like it.

Celeste splashes, moving her soapy body in a turn to face me. She sees me in the mirror also. "Mommy, you scared me!" She speaks with a laugh and I laugh too. Truth is, I am scared but I do not want to show it and we both laugh our nervousness off together. I come into the bathroom and pull the plug, lift her out of the water and wrap her in a big towel. "But Mommy, we didn't wash my hair!" "That's OK."

I don't even argue when Celeste wants to sleep with us. She wedges her little body between Rick and I and it makes me feel better.

The next day, I stare at the half finished manuscript. I wonder if I can do this? I read what I have written and it sounds *blah*. I am still terrified of what I saw last night. It sends my heart racing again. I print the document and try to read it but the pages are all out of order. How does that happen? I wonder if she could have? At least I have numbered them. Shuffling the pages endlessly, I put them in their proper order. As I read, somehow it is still wrong? I realize this isn't good enough. My writing sucks. I struggle to convey the terror that has plagued my life.

Maybe I am not meant to be a writer?

DETERMINED that Charlie will not be on the second floor, Henry decides to check anyway. It is likely he is outside, that's where the chair is- of course he is outside! Wow, how did he miss him? What if he is lying on the ground some-where? Henry can see he is not on the second floor. He has checked every room except for the last bedroom.

There are extra narrow steps that lead to the attic in this room.

Henry has never been to this attic before and he doesn't want to go now.

All he can think about is Wilma and what he heard- the frightful look on her face when they found her... how they found her... He really does not want to go.

"Charlie?"He calls out from the bottom of the narrow stairs.

The lights flicker.

It is more comforting to shout a name, to speak, then to be lost in silent, racing thoughts.

"Charlie?"

Henry puts the fear behind him as his one foot leads the other up the stairs, but the fear wins the race when he reaches the last step. There, Charlie is on the floor. Is he dead? "Charlie!"

He rushes over to him, kneeling down. Drool leaks from Charlie's mouth. "How the hell did you get up here?"

A darkness falls across the attic floor like the shadow of a thunder cloud. The door slams shut! Henry tugs at its handle furiously, his blood now makes the knob slippery from the cuts in his wrist. They are stinging now like someone has poured down vinegar.

12

I t is just before 3 a.m.
I wake up feeling frightened and I don't know why?

Rick is sound asleep snoring loudly beside me. I resent the fact that he can fall asleep so fast, standing up if he had to and yet sometimes it takes me hours. All I can think about is *her. That thing.* It's not even 'a' her.

I don't want to see *her* again.

I am afraid to even walk by a bed. How ridiculous!

I regret meditating and asking her to show me things. Maybe this is the problem? I have done it to myself. You are either crazy or this is just your writer's imagination. I'm sure all writers go through this? I'm sure all writers feel that their characters are real and walking amongst them? Maybe they meet a stranger and think this is so and so, and if this character is real, they would be like them? My thoughts get away from me again. I try to clear my mind and sleep. I think about how I am thinking about not thinking, and around and around it goes. I sigh. How about I concentrate on Rick's peaceful exhales? I try to mimic those. In a constant rhythm it does calm me and I find that I am half asleep.

Until the door opens.

I think it is Celeste. It probably is Celeste.

I am afraid to look.

Any second now and she will pounce on the bed and wedge her little body between us, jabbing me with her elbow. I wait for her to climb on the bed but she doesn't. My feet tingle in anticipation of something that might press down on the blanket.

I dare not to look.

Instead, I look at the alarm clock.

It is 3:12.

I force myself to look.

No one is at the door.

But I heard it creak open?

I see it again. The door. It opens slightly. In any other circumstance something so small wouldn't even phase me, but now, even just a slight movement and it creates a panic of my heart racing to jump inside my throat.

The door opens slightly again.

Could it be a draft? I squint through the darkness and look between the door and its frame. I don't stare for too long in fear that I might see something other than Celeste.

As I pull the covers around my face, buckling down, I see *her*. *That thing.*

There is no denying this.

She is now standing right beside me.

She is looking down on me. *You are not here! You are not here! This is all imaginary.* Even if I don't look, I can feel her. It's a presence- a dread- a knowing, the very kind that makes you tingle. I do not move. I close my eyes. I try to imagine her away. If she exists purely in my imagination, she is not really here and I should be able to imagine her away or imagine myself somewhere else. Heavy upon my chest, it begins. It's a miracle when hollow breaths escape me. Then the pressure moves from my chest, down into my limbs and I am fully aware that I cannot move anything but my eyes. Wow! I can only blink! What is this!

My body is now under her control.

I feel myself lifting.

This is not real! This is not real!

In an instant, I am on the ceiling looking down at Rick in the bed. She is standing below me, arms loosely and relaxed by her side, her face looking upwards with powers able to control me with just her thoughts alone. The walls ignite in flames from the bottom of the baseboards and I see that I am not in my room anymore but surrounded by a circle of wild flames. I am afraid the fire will touch me. It is not hot and I don't feel it burn but it is her flickered breath of fire, her blackened eyes reflecting. I am at her mercy. The release of her rapid thoughts tell me this. Like prey to her fiery web, I am completely helpless. *Death is a mercy.*

I try to scream but nothing comes out. I try to move but I cannot.

And then, she drops me.

I awake before I hit the floor.

I shoot up in bed, screaming! I gasp for air! Rick quickly awakens and turns over to see what is wrong? I realize then that it is just a nightmare but it feels so real! I am relieved and terrified at the same time. I tell Rick what happened while it is still fresh in my mind. I relive the emotions all over again. Patiently he listens as I sob. "Don't you see?" "See what?" "Your dream is showing you- for the book? What happened in the attic." "It is?" "Yes, of course." "You mean that's how their bones are broken?" "Sounds about right to me, don't you think?" I feel good about this. Rick always knows how to inspire me. "Yes, they are dropped from the ceiling." Rick rolls over, he has done his job. "Nothing to be afraid about, it was just a dream, now go back to sleep." Rick's right! It is just a dream. I can write this. This can work... I wonder. It's 3:12 a.m. The door opens? I cling to the naked back of my husband. *Go away! Go away!*

DETERMINED TO WRITE, I work in my dining room again. This time, I know how the story goes; I know what has happened in the attic. The children are home from school but they leave me alone and are in and out of the doorway with their friends, playing mostly outside in the backyard. I immerse myself in the story, feeling even better that they are here.

Wilma is pegged up against the ceiling. I know how terrified she must have been? There are fiery flames below her. She is dropped. All the bones in her body- broken. The same thing happens to Charlie, and the most peculiar, it is exactly six years, six months and six days to the day that Wilma died? 6-6-6? Somehow, Charlie survives. These are the facts I know. I fill in the attic part with my dream. I delete words and rewrite again. They find Charlie lying in the exact same position as Wilma. His bones are broken too but somehow he survives? These injuries equivalent to someone who has fallen from at least three stories?

I think about the little girl, certain that she was neglected and abused in that attic and that she was dropped to her death from the attic's three storey window. I would bet that all her bones were broken too? I want to know her name.

When I look up from typing, I see the back of her.

No, please, no... I don't want to see her. The hairs rise on the back of my neck, and I close my eyes and lock away. *She is not there! She is not there!* All along my legs and arms, I are pimpled. It is the same feeling of dread, the same knowing I had before. It is her presence that is very unnerving. I blink my eyes and look again. Sigh. She is still there. I want to blink her away. *Think of something else! Think of something else!*

She sits outside on the porch swing.

Her back is facing me.

I know it is her because she is wearing the same red dress. They don't make clothes like that anymore.

She knows I am writing about her. We have a rapid understanding conductive through thoughts for this is where she exists in my headspace. *Get a grip, Ramona! This is just your writer's imagination!* I ignore her and keep writing.

The voices of children playing comfort me. Children are so noisy but today I love it. I try to think about happy things, other things, anything but *her*. *No, I do not want to know your name. I have changed my mind.*

In that moment, I am too afraid to write. She is still there. *No! She is not there! She does not exist.* Maybe I should look up some new recipes for dinner?

Celeste rounds the corner to the dining room with a cup of red juice in her hands. She takes a big gulp leaving a red moustache stain on her face. "Who's the girl?" Her curious cuteness in her voice makes me believe that there is a new child around, maybe someone has moved in next door? Maybe Marianne has a new friend over? "What girl?" They are always busy making friends, our doorbell never stops. Celeste points through the large window in the formal living room. I can see it as well from the dining room. "The girl on the porch?"

I don't need to look.

I know exactly what girl she is talking about.

She is there! She is really there!

Terror rips through me like a shot of lightning when I realize that she does exist, that this is not just my writer's imagination, she is actually here in my home. Or is she? "What does she look like?" I turn to ask Celeste. Celeste tilts her head and thoughtfully admires her. "She has long brown hair and a red dress." She says it so simply, like it is an ordinary thing. I am shaking now. I try to hide this. With all the courage I can muster I stand up and take Celeste's hand. "I don't know, let's go look."

We boldly open the front door.

The porch swings empty.

There is no wind and yet it is moving ever so slightly back and forth. We don't see anyone there. Celeste doesn't think anymore about it and passes me her cup. She runs off to play with the other children on the sidewalk. I stand for a minute trying to catch my breath. I am terrified to be in this house! Slowly, I walk back to the dining room. Goosebumps graze my entire body. I look at the screen and think about what I have written there. Screw this! This is beyond anything I am ready for. Rick is wrong, this is not just my writer's imagination! Celeste sees her too! This is not OK!!!

> *I permanently 'shelf' the project.*
> *This time I am sure.*
> *I am too afraid to write it.*

THE LIGHT

13

A year later, I lost someone very close to me in a freak car accident.

It all spiralled down from there.

We found her lifeless body pinned under her car in the garage, shocking and devastating to all that knew her.

The businesses slowly unravelled and profits dwindled; the houses needed to be sold; painful endings with work friends who were not my friends after all; my marriage-hanging by a thread and eventually we called it quits too. Now, a single mother of two preteen daughters, I have to find a way to make it on my own. I feel alone. I am alone! Worthless... depressed in the cold dark of winter, although sometimes when you're depressed you don't know just how depressed you are until you look back, maybe this is a good thing? I hide this from anyone I meet.

One day, it is afternoon. I have no energy. I float in the bathtub, adrift, imagining myself drifting on a lake some-where- anywhere but here. I let the kids do whatever they want so long as they leave me alone, I just can't do this thing they call life anymore. I am still in grief, a hollow existence. It's the grind. It never ends and it is hard. I feel tired of trying hard and not getting anywhere. Financially. Emotionally. In every way. I am angry at Rick. I feel he is not there for me and does not care anymore. I am angry at myself for letting this happen, all the mistakes I have made. I had a plan! Everything was supposed to work accordingly, and yet here I am in the pit of despair, confident that I cannot rise above it.

In the darkness, my soul remains.

If I had friends, I ignored them for fear they would drain me more, which kept me in further isolation, my mind stuck on auto-repeat, the dismal thoughts circling endlessly. How it worked overtime to ensure no hope or strength can return to me. My lifeless body floated on a sea of tears, my fingertips wrinkled and worn, the water cold and filthy- I am one with it.

The bathroom light is off and I pull the shower curtain along the edges of the tub as if to hide myself there. *I will never be able to rebuild my life. I am alone. I am helpless. No one would want me now with two kids that are not their blood... I am not worthy... No one loves me. I am not lovable.* Over and over this repeats. I realize now that these are lies from the darkness. I don't know how to guard my mind and so it continues, creating the emotions of despair behind it. When the water circles the drain and I have no water pity to submerge myself in, I resist climbing out because that will mean that I will have to get dressed and go back to real life. I hate my life. I would rather just float here. I shiver without the water. Why did I pull the drain? Just because it is cold, my nipples tell me it is colder now. I imagine being small enough to slip through the drain with the dirty bath water. What a relief it would be to not have to try anymore.

I hear the passing laughter of my children in the hallway. They have no idea how I feel. Their innocence, their childhood, their happiness of a simple stress free life; how I have worked so hard to make it all so very magical for them. How much would it mess up their life if that illusion was not there? The thought breaks me down and I weep. I would never take my own life but in those moments, I can certainly understand the pain of why someone might want to. It is heart wrenching. I climb out of the tub. I clean myself up and go back into the world again. I don't know how I do it. I don't know if there is a God. I do not know God. What is the purpose of this? *Somehow, I go on.*

Sometime later, I bump into someone whom I had met years before. Being on a trial separation, I size up any man as potential to the happy family I so desperately wanted. My interest in him is less than noble and he is a man that I cannot easily seduce, and this intrigues me. Like a moth to a flame, I am attracted to him and I realize now that it is his *light* that I am attracted to. It radiates in his eyes, so full of love and peace, a very strong man of faith. I want that.

He invited me to join him with a group of friends one night. Gladly, I accept. I take this as a possibility that he might like me. My daughters are welcome to come and they can play with their children. I have no idea what I am in for. These people are Evangelical Christians. This is a weekly prayer meeting that they hold in their home every Thursday night. This is not a date. This is not? Well, just go with it... but I know he is single and looking for a wife, someone has mentioned to me. I am here to be saved by a man only to hear about a man that has already done this for me- his name is Jesus Christ. He died on the cross to save me. Did I get that right? This is a girl who once laughed hysterically when I thought about placing a large billboard sign in the Mennonite fields near my home with a sign that read, "F**k Jesus" right next to theirs. For some reason, the thought of this was hilarious to me, and yet here I am, possibly with Bible holding Mennonites among us. They love me anyway. I do not share these things. If I did, I am sure they would love me anyway, they are just that kind. I find I start to like these people and I feel better when I leave, so much in fact, that I can't wait to return next Thursday, counting down the days.

As the weeks go by, I learn more about faith.

We meet new people from all walks of life and I get to hear their stories. I do not share mine.

I like this living room. It is nice how they have decorated it. The couch is so comfortable. They have snacks. Mmmm-this is good. What is this? Someone brings out a guitar and it feels like a warm gathering of friends. Someone even privately shares that they have been able to cut down on their antidepressant medication since they have attended this group, under doctor supervision of course, and I wonder if that is why he brought me here? Does he think I need to be on medication? Do I seem depressed? I am really not. Maybe he isn't interested in me at all? I am not good enough.

One night, a young man from India visited. He is now Christian, a musician for which I bought his music CD, and he played for us. I love this stuff! I soon learned that he has prophetic gifts, not just musical gifts. He has the unique ability to see or know things. As this young man moved around the room, he stopped at each person to share a special message just for them. Some of my friends have been praying for things and I am amazed when he speaks to them about things that are relevant to them, whether in a bible verse or in a vision he sees. Every message is so different but all happy, and they are thrilled by what he has told them. Some of us are strangers so I find this interesting.

And then, he stops at me.

I am the last one.

I am OK if he wants to skip over and call it a night?

His face grows very serious and it makes me nervous.

"You were in a dark place recently."

He doesn't say this like it is a question, he speaks it as if it is a statement of truth. I smile and laugh it off.

"OK?" - Like, no? I don't know what you're talking about?

He doesn't smile. He is sure about this 'dark place' despite my efforts to convince him otherwise.

"I see water. You were in water."

I start to feel embarrassed and dart my eyes around the room. I felt exposed. How could he know this? No one knows. Again, he states this. It is not a question. Now I am really nervous because I don't know what else he is going to say. I know he is speaking truth as he explains intimate details about how I was feeling that one very day. *It was my bathtub moment,* when I questioned the world and my existence in it.

When he looks at me, it feels as if he is peering into my soul.

> *"Jesus just wants you to know that He was with you at that time."*

That was it! That is my message- "Jesus just wants you to know that He was with you at that time." The words choke me up and I try to hold back the tears. Wait? Jesus sees me?

Does he really see us? He loves me? He is with me? It is beautiful. It makes me cry. I feel truly loved and cared for. I repeat the words: "*Jesus just wants you to know that He was with you at that time.*"

I guess a man really did come to save me.

14

One night while lying in bed, my right eye went completely dark. I was staring up at the ceiling, thinking about things when suddenly it was as if someone had flicked off the light switch. I could only see out of my left eye, even in the dark one can see some. I was terrified. I turned on the light to confirm. Yes, only my left eye could see light, the other eye remained in complete darkness. Tears clouded my limited vision as I thought about the possibility that I was now completely blind in the one eye. I could not imagine.

Ten minutes later, full vision returned. It happened again about a month later. This time it only lasted for about six long minutes. I arranged for an eye appointment and immediately was referred to a specialist. They also sent me to the hospital for tests and through the process of elimination, they checked the veins in my neck and in my heart with an ultrasound to see if there were any blockages.

I shared my ordeal about my sight with my friends on a Thursday evening and that I had a follow up appointment the next day. We had so many people there that night, the living room so full that it was hard to even find a seat. My cell phone rang and I had to go, work was calling. While at the door, the friend I liked met me there. "I want to pray over your eyes before you go." "I am seeing the doctor tomorrow, don't worry about it." "Ramona, let me pray." He extended his hand over my right eye and snapped his fingers with his other hand, speaking against the spirit of blindness and commanding it to leave in the *name of Jesus.* "Ya, ya, ya, ya," I said, while putting on my shoes. All I could think about was work and the customers that were waiting for me. I did not care about his silly little prayer.

When I went to the doctors the next day, my eye specialist was rummaging through my file, all the charts and papers strung astray. He would roll the small black stool he sat on towards the computer and then back again to look at the paperwork like he had missed something? This went on for some time. "Is everything OK?" He scratches his head of science. "It must be a misdiagnosis? I don't understand it, your eye is perfect today." I am amazed and give a slight chuckle- "Really?" "Really." I tell him that someone had prayed over it the night before and maybe God had healed it? It felt stupid to say this especially speaking to a man who has built his life around science and perhaps not faith, but he simply smiled and said, "I believe you." I was discharged that day. I haven't had a problem with my vision since.

Growing deeper in my faith, I travelled to Oakville for a conference at The Meeting House. It was a yearly event called Fluid, for young people to come together to learn about Christianity and worship in musical praise. I was surprised to see so many young faces and so much interest in God? When I was that age I was interested in worldly things- not God. This is amazing! In the next few hours, we heard miraculous stories and speeches from those who had been changed by faith. It made me realize how much one needs faith in order to navigate through our broken world.

Raising my hands or keeping them open, I sang in musical worship, closing my eyes and feeling the Holy Spirit move. I felt a tingle in my hands. I didn't think much about this until driving home, my hands wrapped around the steering wheel while looking down at them. They were not tingling anymore but I had a revelation- one can have many revelations while driving alone. I realized that the tingling sensation was in the exact same spot where the nails may have been spiked into the flesh of Jesus Christ when he was crucified on the cross. It was close to the wrist area, but just above, at the base of the palm. I wept, gripping my hands around the wheel, in awe of what the Holy Spirit has shown me. I knew the spot! How Jesus suffered with such selfless love for us.

"For this is how God loved the world:
He gave his one and only Son,
so that everyone who believes in Him,
will not perish but have eternal life."
John 3:16

15

I don't feel the ghost of her anymore- evil spirit or whatever *that thing* was. She no longer haunts me and for this I am glad. Even as I write this, I feel evil has no power over me. I no longer live in fear. I am certain of a God that loves me. I have been changed by His love for me.

On an August long weekend in 2015,
I received my biggest miracle yet.

Three days prior, I had prayed to God and asked Him if He is real? Is the speaking of tongues and the healings and all the rest of it real? I didn't want to be led down a path that was not of God. I asked for discernment, in Christian language, and if this indeed was a real thing, could I please know more of God. It is the most sincere prayer I could have made. It only took a few minutes to speak in my mind and fold my hands, and then I forgot about it. This was a late Thursday evening.

On a beautiful Sunday afternoon, I was sitting on my back patio. I looked up and saw a shining light. A friend has emailed me a worship song- *"Holy of Holies" by Paul Wilbur* because they knew how much I loved music. There is a story in the music video, he explained, so I clicked the link on my phone and let the music pour into my ears through headphones.

On the second verse, The Light appeared..

It is nothing of this world and for this I am certain and bewildered. I stare at it in beautiful amazement wondering where it came from? It dazzles me how it dances before me, so bright like the reflection off water. It is nearly blinding. I study it and can see that it is in the shape of a sliding trapezoid figure. This puzzles me because if it was light from the sun shining through leaves, it would not have these kinds of edges.

Without warning, *The Light* cascades down and moves towards me. It enters my body swiftly, first my throat and chest area and I burn *hot hot hot!* I can't believe this! I feel it take root in the pit of my stomach, like some kind of base. I like to think of it like I had swallowed an acorn, it is about that size. Although I feel like it has been there all along, I am just feeling it now, it is coming alive. When I look down, I am glowing. I stretch out my fingers. They are glowing too! I wonder if I will die because the fire inside me is burning so intensely? Isn't there something called spontaneous human combustion? *I burn and burn and burn* but not in a painful way, peace blankets me. It is a peace I never knew existed. Slowly, the burn fades. The song has long finished.

Quickly, I called my friend. I wanted to tell him what just happened. He is amazed and tells me that he felt God nudge him to send me the link. I no longer feel anything but peace. Thoughts about work, people, worries, stress, life-completely gone. I am so joyful! I cannot explain it. Even my closest family notices- "I don't know what happened to you, but you are very different." "Like how different?" "Like calm." I have never felt an inner peace like this in my life and did not know this was even possible. Still to this day, I long for this intensity of peace to blanket me.

When speaking with my faith friends the very next Thursday, I told them what had happened. I didn't care what people thought, I know what happened to me. My father tells me not to tell anyone as he believes I sound crazy. But I tell everyone! How could I not share the most beautiful spiritual encounter of my life? In the Bible, John was also a witness to *The Light!*

My faith friends are not surprised like I thought they would be. "It sounds like you have been baptized by fire." Unanimously, they agree. Baptized by fire? What is that? They tell me to read The Bible. Red face, it is true, I do not know The Bible like they do. I look there for reference. They helped me find it. "You mean this is real?" They laugh. For some reason, the gravity of The Bible being absolute truth was not something that I fully accepted until that moment. Somehow, it came alive to me. There are so many references to *The Light*. I take this as an answer to my prayer.

Now, whenever I hear preaching or sometimes in musical worship, I can feel the Holy Spirit burn in my chest and stomach. It is not of the same intensity as that Sunday afternoon in August, but it is still there burning within me.

(Does anyone else know what I am talking about? If you have the same burn, I would sure love to hear from you.)

There is evil, and there is God.
There is darkness, and there is *Light*.
I think I have seen both.

I didn't write this book to write about evil, but to write about how I have overcome it. I am no different or more special than you. He has given me is a gift to see The Light, but he giving you a gift to believe it. This is the gift of salvation.

IN THIS DREAM, I MET JESUS

I died in a car accident on the 401 Highway. (*I sure hope this isn't going to happen!*)

The sky was completely dark and I was among stars that were crashing down all around me. There was a huge red moon before it went dark. It felt very scary and unsettling. In the distance, I saw a Light and it came closer and larger. It was Jesus. He met me in the sky and we were floating about six feet apart. He knew who I was and knew everything about me. I was aware that I had died. He knew my name. He didn't speak but we could communicate through thoughts.

When he touched my shoulder, I turned into a great big seven foot angel! I was immediately aware that I was a part of a wide network of angels that stretched across the sky from the east end to the west. I could see the angels arching over the horizon. There were so many of us and I was excited to be a part of this angel network. At that moment, it was not about me anymore. I did not have a family. My old life had died and I belonged to Him now. I had no regrets and this is what I wanted. I felt so honoured to serve Him, I cannot even explain the intensity of what this felt like to serve Him. This emotion remained with me long after I woke up.

I told a friend about my dream. They seemed very interested in some of the elements I described.

They opened their Bible to Mathew 24:29.

As they read the words, it sure did sound similar.

I was embarrassed to admit that I had never read that passage before.

This amazed them even more!

Excerpt from The Bible: (Matthew 24:29-31)

"Immediately after the tribulation of those days shall the sun be darkened and the moon shall not give her light, and the stars shall fall from heaven, and the powers of the heavens shall be shaken; And then shall appear the sign of the Son of man in heaven: and then shall all the tribes of earth mourn, and they shall see the Son of man coming in the clouds of heaven with power and great glory. And he shall send his angels with a great sound of trumpet, and they shall gather together in his elect from the four winds, from one end of heaven to the other."

In the dream, Jesus told me that I would save millions of lives. I have no idea what this means.

My assignment- the building. It was late at night and I was on the night watch! Perched at the side of it, on the corner, I guarded near the rooftop with my large white angel wings hovering. The building had Roman-like pillars and was a historical icon. There were city streets all around it but there one just one cobblestone street, and that's what I looked down on. It also had a freestanding black clock. The streets were covered in spiritual darkness and that is why I was there.

Years later, in real life, I arrived at this building. I recognized it right away because I had dreamed it so explicitly. At this place, I started a new job, nothing related to ministry work. Ironically, I work the night shift. I don't know why God has brought me to Union Station or how long I will be there, but I find it amazing that I had dreamed about this building before I even saw it.

I have created a new life for myself there and have made wonderful friendships with people I would have not otherwise met.

The only thing that haunts this *Haunted Writer*, is how my story will end. But, I guess He has it all figured out.

I fell on my knees and humbled myself, asking God for forgiveness, for my unbelief, and everything else.

I begged Him to restore my marriage... and He did.

*Charlie Livingston spent months in hospital care
after he was found lying unconscious in the attic.*

*Once released, he returned to the old farmhouse where he resides
to this day.*
*He still claims that he is innocent in the death and murder of his
wife, Wilma.*

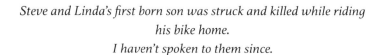

Steve and Linda's first born son was struck and killed while riding his bike home.
I haven't spoken to them since.

"When Jesus spoke again to the people, he said,

"I am the Light of the world.
Whoever follows me will never walk in darkness,
but will have the light of life."
John 8:12

Reference:

- *Derek Prince, Deliverance Ministry: www. derekprince.org*
- *Jacob Wells Ministry, Deliverance Teachings and Workshops, www.jacobswellministries.ca*
- *The Journey, A Christian Church, www. myjourney.ca*
- *Community Christian Reformed Church, www.ccrc. on.ca*
- *Conference: www.fluidgathering.com*
- David Wilkinson Music, David JW "Give Me Jesus" https://youtu.be/75FQAmKSH08
- *Billy Graham.org, Billy Graham Christian Ministry*
- *The Holy Bible, www.biblegateway.com*
- *https://www.youtube.com/watch?v=s4CRvAPzxjI*
- *Song: "For Your Name is Holy, Holy of Holies," By Paul Wilbur.*

Our Father who art in heaven,
Hallowed be thy name;
Thy kingdom come;
Thy will be done;
On earth as it is in heaven.
Give us this day our daily bread,
And forgive us our trespasses,
As we forgive those who trespass
    against us.
And lead us not into temptation;
But deliver us from evil.
For thine is the kingdom.
The power and the glory,
Forever and ever,
Amen.

Matthew 6:9-13

Manufactured by Amazon.ca
Bolton, ON

21057935R00061